Governing the United States

Ask a Congressperson

Christy Mihaly

ROurke
Educational Media
rourkeeducationalmedia.com

A Division of
Carson
Dellosa
Education

BEFORE AND DURING READING ACTIVITIES

Before Reading: *Building Background Knowledge and Vocabulary*

Building background knowledge can help children process new information and build upon what they already know. Before reading a book, it is important to tap into what children already know about the topic. This will help them develop their vocabulary and increase their reading comprehension.

Questions and Activities to Build Background Knowledge:

1. Look at the front cover of the book and read the title. What do you think this book will be about?
2. What do you already know about this topic?
3. Take a book walk and skim the pages. Look at the table of contents, photographs, captions, and bold words. Did these text features give you any information or predictions about what you will read in this book?

Vocabulary: *Vocabulary Is Key to Reading Comprehension*

Use the following directions to prompt a conversation about each word.

- Read the vocabulary words.
- What comes to mind when you see each word?
- What do you think each word means?

Vocabulary Words:
- bills
- committees
- constituents
- district
- hearings
- legislative
- represents
- staff

During Reading: *Reading for Meaning and Understanding*

To achieve deep comprehension of a book, children are encouraged to use close reading strategies. During reading, it is important to have children stop and make connections. These connections result in deeper analysis and understanding of a book.

Close Reading a Text

During reading, have children stop and talk about the following:

- Any confusing parts
- Any unknown words
- Text to text, text to self, text to world connections
- The main idea in each chapter or heading

Encourage children to use context clues to determine the meaning of any unknown words. These strategies will help children learn to analyze the text more thoroughly as they read.

When you are finished reading this book, turn to the next-to-last page for **Text-Dependent Questions** and an **Extension Activity**.

TABLE OF CONTENTS

What Is a Congressperson?

Your congressperson speaks for you in the government of the United States. How? Ask a congressperson!

What is a congressperson's job?

Congresspeople are members of Congress. They make laws for the country. Each congressperson **represents** the people in their **district**. Members of Congress are elected by the people. Citizens vote for the person they believe will do the best job for their community.

How does someone become a congressperson?

A congressperson must be at least 25 years old. They must be a U.S. citizen for at least seven years. They must live in the state they represent.

They serve for two years. To stay in Congress, they have to win an election again.

Congresspeople work in the U.S. Capitol Building in Washington, D.C.

Why are congresspeople important?

Congresspeople are part of the **legislative** branch of the government. The legislative branch is responsible for making the country's laws. These laws set the rules for paying taxes, becoming a citizen, protecting the environment, making sure our food is safe, and many other important things.

Congressperson Veronica Escobar of Texas supports background checks for gun purchases to keep her district safe.

Laws begin as ideas. These ideas are presented as **bills**.

Congresspeople vote on bills. If enough people vote "yes," a bill will pass Congress.

What does a congressperson do at work?

Members of Congress have a busy schedule. They meet with their **staff**. They read mail and follow the news. They meet with community members and attend meetings about bills, concerns, and ideas. They meet with other congresspeople who have the same beliefs.

A congressperson travels and gives speeches. They meet with people who live in their district—their **constituents**—to let them know about the work they are doing to make the community a better place.

What Is the House of Representatives?

What happens in the House?

The House of Representatives is not a building. It is the group of 435 congresspeople who represent districts all over the country. Members of the House come together to discuss bills and to vote.

The House of Representatives meets in this chamber of the Capitol Building in Washington, D.C.

Salud Carbajal
Represents 24th district,
California

Adriano Espaillat
Represents 13th district,
New York

Pramila Jayapal
Represents 7th district,
Washington

Debbie Mucarsel-Powell
Represents 26th district,
Florida

Ilhan Omar
Represents 5th district,
Minnesota

Albio Sires
Represents 8th district,
New Jersey

Who's in the House?

The House is diverse. It includes people with many different backgrounds and points of view.

How does the House study bills?

Members of the House meet in smaller groups to discuss bills. These **committees** focus on different issues that are important to the country.

Eighteen-year-old Ethan Lindenberger shares opinions with Congress during a committee hearing.

President Barack Obama meets with members of Congress.

Committees hold **hearings**. People talk during committee hearings. They give their opinions on bills. Experts come to speak. People who will be affected by new laws give their ideas too. Committee members ask questions.

How does a bill become a law?

Eventually, a bill that has passed Congress goes to the president. If the president signs a bill, it becomes a law.

President Ronald Reagan

Student Interns
These young high school and college students learn about Congress by becoming interns.

Who runs the House?

The person in charge is the Speaker of the House. The Speaker is a congressperson elected by House members. The Speaker decides what bills the House will talk about.

Speaker of the House Nancy Pelosi

Congress is changing to include people who were not equally represented in the past. For example, there were 102 women elected to the House in 2018. That is the most ever.

Interesting Facts About a Congressperson

Where does a congressperson live?

Many congresspeople have families. Their families often stay in their district. House members can go home on weekends. But they need someplace to sleep in Washington, D.C.

What benefits does a congressperson get?

Members of Congress travel often. They get free parking at airports around Washington, D.C. Their travel is often paid for.

House members can go to a gym that is just for Congress. They get offices near the Capitol Building. A tunnel connects some offices to the Capitol. Members ride an underground train between buildings.

In order to do their job, your congressperson needs to know what people need and want.

Your congressperson wants to know your views. Tell them what you think!

Government of the United States

Your congressperson is a member of the House of Representatives. Can you find where they fit into this chart?

	Legislative Branch Makes the laws.	**Executive Branch** Carries out the laws.	**Judicial Branch** Decides what laws mean.
Federal Governs the whole country.	**Congress** Includes Senators and members of the House of Representatives.	**The President** Works with cabinet members such as the U.S. Attorney General.	**U.S. Courts** Judges work at many courts, including the U.S. Supreme Court.
State Governs each of the 50 states.	**State Legislature** Representatives work at the capitol building in each state's capital city.	**The Governor** Works with many officials such as the Secretary of State and the State Attorney General.	**State Courts** Include the highest court in the state— the state Supreme Court.
Local Governs each village, town, or city.	**City Council** Representatives make rules about how land is used, where roads will be built, and more.	**The City Mayor** Is in charge of the police department, the parks department, and more.	**Local Courts** Judges rule on cases that involve city laws and crimes that are less serious.

Glossary

bills (bilz): rough copies or drafts of ideas for new laws

committees (kuh-MI-teez): groups of people within a legislature that hold hearings and vote on proposed bills

constituents (kuhn-STI-chuh-wuhnts): people who agree to let a representative speak for them

district (DIS-trikt): an area or region, as in the congressional district represented by a congressperson

hearings (HEER-ingz): formal meetings that give people a chance for their opinions to be heard

legislative (LEJ-is-lay-tiv): relating to the branch of government that makes new laws

represents (rep-ri-ZENTS): speaks or acts for someone else

staff (staf): a group of people working for a boss or organization

Index

Text-Dependent Questions

1. How do congresspeople find out what people in their districts want and need?

2. What do House committees do?

3. What do committee members do at a hearing?

4. Who has the power to sign a bill into law?

5. If you met your congressperson, what is one question you would ask?

Extension Activity

Who is your congressperson? If you don't know, look it up. Try this website: https://www.house.gov/representatives/find-your-representative. Find your congressperson's website. Read about what your congressperson is working on. Check how to contact them. Call their office or send an email or letter. Tell them about a problem or share an idea for improving things in your district, state, or country.

ABOUT THE AUTHOR

Christy Mihaly is the author of nonfiction and informational books for young readers, including a picture book about the First Amendment, *Free for You and Me*. She worked as an attorney for many years. She lives in Vermont, which has just one (very hard-working) congressperson for the whole state. Find out more or say hello at Christy's website: www.christymihaly.com.

www.rourkeeducationalmedia.com

PHOTO CREDITS: cover: ©YayaErnst; page 4: ©SPI Productions; page 5: ©zrfphoto; page 6: ©Tom Williams; page 7: ©franckreporter; page 8: ©FatCamera; page 9: ©Marcos Calvo; page 10: ©wikipedia; page 11: ©Erin Granzow, ©Lean Hermn, ©Erin Connolly, ©Franmarie Metzler, ©Kristie Boyd, U.S. Congress; page 12: ©Zuma Press; page 13: ©Pete Souza; page 14: ©Mark Reinstein; page 15: ©French Hill; page 16: ©Aaron-Schwartz; page 17: ©Kristie Boyd; page 18, 19: ©Architect of the Capitol; page 20: ©triloks

Edited by: Madison Capitano
Cover design by: Rhea Magaro-Wallace
Interior design by: Janine Fisher

Library of Congress PCN Data

Ask a Congressperson / Christy Mihaly (Governing the United States)
ISBN 978-1-73162-911-1 (hard cover)
ISBN 978-1-73162-910-4 (soft cover)
ISBN 978-1-73162-912-8 (e-Book)
ISBN 978-1-73163-349-1 (ePub)
Library of Congress Control Number: 2019944959

Rourke Educational Media
Printed in the United States of America,
North Mankato, Minnesota